THE BEAR
DETECTIVES

For James Fernandes,
who listened to me telling stories
on October 13, 2008
S.G.

For Toby
J.B.

ORCHARD BOOKS
338 Euston Road, London NW1 3BH
Orchard Books Australia
Hachette Children's Books
Level 17/207 Kent Street, Sydney NSW 2000

First published by Orchard Books in 2009
First paperback publication in 2010

Text © Sally Grindley 2009
Illustrations © Jo Brown 2009

The rights of Sally Grindley to be identified as the author and
Jo Brown to be identified as the illustrator of this work
have been asserted by them in accordance with the
Copyright, Designs and Patents Act, 1988.

ISBN 978 1 84616 108 7 (hardback)
ISBN 978 1 84616 158 2 (paperback)

1 3 5 7 9 10 8 6 4 2 (hardback)
1 3 5 7 9 10 8 6 4 2 (paperback)

Printed in China

Orchard Books is a division of Hachette Children's Books,
an Hachette UK company.

www.hachette.co.uk

Treasure Hunt

Written by **SALLY GRINDLEY**
Illustrated by **JO BROWN**

ORCHARD BOOKS

Constable Tiggs

Sergeant Bumble

The judges

One day, Sergeant Bumble
and Constable Tiggs found
a notice pinned to a tree on
the village green. It read:

Treasure
Hunt

"A treasure hunt!" said Tiggs excitedly. "Can we join in?"
"I'm so good at solving clues, it wouldn't be fair to everybody else," said Bumble. "But you can join in, Constable Tiggs."

Later that day, villagers gathered
on the green, waiting for the
treasure hunt to begin.

The organiser handed out some sheets of paper. "The first team to solve all the clues will win a big box of chocolates," she said.

"Chocolates, eh?" said Bumble. "I'll just have a look at the first clue." He took the sheet of paper from Tiggs. "*When the wind blows, watch this bird turn*," he read.

"What birds can you think of?"
Bumble asked.

"Ducks? Hens? Robins?" suggested
Tiggs.

"Ducks, that's the answer," said
Bumble. "They're always turning
round and round on the pond.
Write it down, Constable Tiggs."

Tiggs didn't seem very sure. Then suddenly he cried, "Look up there!" Bumble looked where Tiggs was pointing. "It's a weather vane," he said.

"Look what's on the weather vane," said Tiggs.

"It's a cockerel," said Bumble.

"That's the answer," said Tiggs.

"Is it?" said Bumble.

"When the wind blows it makes the cockerel turn," said Tiggs. "Of course," nodded Bumble. "That's just what I was going to say."

"Let me help you with one
more clue," said Bumble.
Tiggs read out the next one.
"What's green under a woolly jumper?"

"We'd better look in our
wardrobes," said Bumble.

They ran back to the police house.
The only green thing they could
find under their jumpers was a
scarf. "That must be the answer,"
said Bumble.

Tiggs looked very thoughtful.
"I think the answer is grass,"
he said.
"There's no grass in my
wardrobe," argued Bumble.
"I think it's a trick question,"
said Tiggs. "A woolly jumper is a
lamb, because a lamb is covered
in wool and jumps about on
grass. And grass is green!"

"Well, if they're going to ask silly questions," said Bumble, "I shall go home and have a cup of tea."

"Please stay and help. It's the last question," pleaded Tiggs. "The clue is, *What flying creature might be related to Sergeant Bumble?*...

...you're in the clue, Sir!"

"So I am," said Bumble importantly.

"Let's sit down so that I can think."

They sat on a bench.

Bumble started to think.
"I've thought about
all of my relations,"
he said at last,
"but none of them
can fly. If I don't
know the answer,
nobody else will
either, so we
can miss that
clue out."

Suddenly, there was a loud
buzzing noise.

Something big and black and
yellow flew out of the bushes and
landed on Bumble's nose.

Bumble leapt to his feet and tried
to brush it off. It landed on his ear.
"Get off!" he boomed. He started
to run away, flapping
his paws at it.

"That's it, that's the answer," cried
Tiggs. "Come back, Sergeant
Bumble. I know the answer!"
Bumble was too far away to hear.

Tiggs waited and waited
for him, but he didn't
come back.

At last, Tiggs wrote down his
answer on the sheet of paper
and took it to the judges.

As soon as the judging was over, he rushed back to the police house.

Hunt

Bumble was dozing in a chair.
"Wake up, Sergeant Bumble," said
Tiggs excitedly.

"Eh, what?" Bumble muttered.
"We won!" Tiggs said.
He held out the big box
of chocolates.

"Bumble bee! That was the
answer, and I would never
have got it without you."

"Of course," nodded Bumble.
"I am very clever. Now, which
chocolate shall I have first?"

THE BEAR DETECTIVES

SALLY GRINDLEY 🐾 JO BROWN

Bucket Rescue	978 1 84616 152 0
Who Shouted Boo?	978 1 84616 109 4
The Ghost Train	978 1 84616 153 7
Treasure Hunt	978 1 84616 108 7
The Mysterious Earth	978 1 84616 155 1
The Strange Pawprint	978 1 84616 156 8
The Missing Spaghetti	978 1 84616 157 5
A Very Important Day	978 1 84616 154 4

All priced at £8.99

Orchard Colour Crunchies are available from all good bookshops,
or can be ordered direct from the publisher:
Orchard Books, PO BOX 29, Douglas IM99 1BQ
Credit card orders please telephone 01624 836000
or fax 01624 837033 or visit our website: www.orchardbooks.co.uk
or e-mail: bookshop@enterprise.net for details.

To order please quote title, author and ISBN
and your full name and address.
Cheques and postal orders should be made payable to 'Bookpost plc.'
Postage and packing is FREE within the UK
(overseas customers should add £2.00 per book).

Prices and availability are subject to change.